Trapped on Dinosaur Island!

by Dave Villager

First edition (June 2022)

Book cover art © 2022, Florian Garbay

Pawkins Publishing 2022

CHAPTER ONE

Jenny really thought a special school trip to a remote Scottish island would change her life. After all, only two kids from her school of over fifteen hundred students had been selected to be part of this trip, and she was one of them. Surely, the trip would offer some amazing lessons, scenery, and experiences.

But so far, the scenery was the only thing she'd gotten excited about. The fields and stretches of scant forests were beautiful, made of shades of green she would have never even known existed had she not come on the trip. And the beaches reminded her of the golden and seemingly impossible stretches of sand and sea she'd sometimes seen on the walls of dentist offices and laptop wallpapers.

It was a shame all that beauty was overshadowed by just how *boring* the place was. Jenny was standing on a large, flat rock with eleven other students. They all looked directly ahead, where a teacher who looked to be roughly five hundred years old was telling them all about how moss formations had managed to thrive on the island for centuries. His name was Dr. Gaunt, and he was very excited about moss, dirt, and rocks.

"I think maybe this guy has also thrived on the island for centuries," said a voice from beside her. Jenny turned and saw her best friend, Ahmed, chuckling behind his hand. It had really worked out well that Ahmed had been the second student from her school to be approved for the trip. At least with him here, she'd have a few laughs.

The joke went unheard by the other students— selections from other schools back home in England. Most of them also seemed to be very bored. Jenny figured that the other ten kids were here for the same reason she and Ahmed had applied for the trip. They had a deep interest in science, were the top-performing students in their schools, and thought the idea of staying five days on a beautiful Scottish isle sounded like a blast.

And now here they were, listening to Dr. Gaunt discuss how Scottish thread-moss was very adaptive to most tropical climates. "Ah, yes, and one more thing," he said, delighted and speaking as if he'd forgotten he had an audience of kids standing in front of him. "Did you know that there are around one thousand different varieties of moss and liverwort in Scotland? And more than one hundred of them exist here on Grovey Island. Now, come this way, and we may even be able to get a glimpse of the infamous Grovey slugs!"

Dr. Gaunt waved them forward as he hobbled down a narrow dirt path. The path wound through a thick grove of trees and weeds, leading them up a slight hill that seemed to promise more greenery.

"Did you hear that, Jenny?" Ahmed said. "We may get to see *slugs!*"

"Oh, I heard. I can barely contain my excitement."

Snickering together, the pair remained near the back of the group. Jenny did have to admit that the island had its charms. The towering trees were gigantic compared to the trees in her hometown. And certain parts of Grovey Island made her feel like she was on another planet, with its weird rock formations and strange plants.

Dr. Gaunt stopped the group at a flat expanse of ground. Hills rolled perfectly in the distance; the sort of curvy hills children draw with bright green crayons. Dr. Gaunt hunkered down on his knees, both of which popped on his way down. He dug into the ground with his fingers and shook his head.

"Alas, I don't think we'll be seeing any Grovey slugs today. Soil's too moist."

"Oh no," Jenny said quietly. "That just ruins the whole trip!"

A girl beside her heard this. She rolled her eyes and tutted at Jenny.

"Oh, well," Dr. Gaunt said. "I suppose I can just tell you about them, and of course, they'll be featured in the slideshow when we return to the conference center."

"What a relief," Ahmed joked. "We can...woah. Jenny, do you see that?"

He was pointing ahead and to the right. Jenny followed the direction his finger was pointing but saw nothing but the rolling hills in the distance. However, she then saw the shape of a very tall building on the other side of the hills. Jenny had nearly missed it because it appeared to be made completely of glass, reflecting the blue sky overhead. She thought it might be quite tall, but it was hard to tell because of the hills and the distance. She figured it had to be at least a mile or two away.

Now that she saw it, it was all she could really notice about the landscape. It was a remarkable building, but it also looked very out of place on Grovey

Island.

"Yeah," Jenny said. "I wonder what it is."

Grinning devilishly, Ahmed raised his hand. "Excuse me, Dr. Gaunt?"

The old man looked up from his digging, peering through thick glasses at Ahmed. He looked thrilled to have a question from the crowd. "Yes? Yes, son, did you have a question?"

"What's that big building over there?" He pointed in the direction of the tall, glass building.

Dr. Gaunt frowned. Jenny got the impression he already knew where Ahmed was pointing, and he didn't want to answer. Still, he was more or less trapped now, as all twelve students were glaring at him.

"Ah, that, that... yes, that's the um... well, that's just the processing center for the island. Yes, that's what it is. All of the specimens we find here on the island that aren't found anywhere else on the mainland are taken there to be processed, listed, and studied."

A little murmur of conversation passed through the group as Dr. Gaunt got back to his feet. Once again, his knees popped as he started back down the trail he'd just led them through. To Jenny, it seemed that he was

suddenly in a hurry to get them away from the field—
and not just because he'd not been able to find any of
his precious slugs.

"Come now," he said. "If we make it back to the
conference center in time, we should get first choice
for dinner!"

There was some hooting and clapping of
excitement at this. It had, after all, been a very long
day of trekking and exploring Grovey Island, and
everyone had grown hungry. The idea of an early
dinner had even put some extra speed into Jenny and
Ahmed as they meandered back down the trail.

Yet as they walked through the trees and headed
back to the center of the island, Jenny looked back to
that large, glass building. It truly did seem out of place,
and Dr. Gaunt had clearly not wanted to answer
questions about it.

What is that place? Jenny wondered. *What is it,
really?*

And with that thought in her head, she decided
that maybe Grovey Island wasn't so boring after all.

CHAPTER TWO

They headed back to their hotel in a small bus as the sun started to set over the sea. Jenny looked out at the sunlight reflecting off the water, once again struck by just how beautiful Grovey Island was. It sure was a shame that the trip had been such a snoozefest.

The bus was very nice, not the plain sort that carried her to school in the mornings. The seats were polished, and the entire bus smelled clean. There wasn't even chewing gum under the seats. This, plus the gorgeous scenery just outside her window, made Jenny feel like she was on holiday. Which, she supposed, she was. Not every kid who'd wanted to come to Grovey Island had been able to go on this trip. Jenny knew that she and Ahmed were part of a special, select group, so she supposed she should be more grateful.

"So," Ahmed said beside her. "Are you homesick yet?"

"Ahmed, it's only been one day."

"I know. But still…it's hard to be away from family."

"Are *you* homesick?"

"Not yet. I think I will be at dinner. My mom is a great cook. I think I'll start missing home when I can't have dinner at my own kitchen table."

"I think for me, it will come when it's time to go to bed. I have problems sleeping in strange places." This was true. Even when she spent the occasional weekend at her grandparents' house, Jenny always had problems falling asleep.

"Maybe things will get a little better once we get past all these lectures on moss and dirt," Ahmed suggested.

"Yeah, maybe."

She looked back out the window and noticed that the road was curving. They were coming to an area of the island where the land rose up as they went further inland, and the sea seemed to fall away. Instead of open fields and spectacular sea views, she saw a vast forest. This was one of the many appealing things about Grovey Island; it had such a diverse environment. There were so many different biomes to study—from the sea to the forests, to the small swampy areas to the large, open fields.

As the bus continued further inland, the forest came to an end. Without the rising trees to block her view, Jenny could once again see the vague shape of that large building way out on the other side of the island. Now that she'd been able to clearly see it while on their moss excursion, she could spot it easily, even when it was reflecting the sky so perfectly that the building didn't seem to be there at all.

Only, it was a bit easier to see now. The setting sun was casting bronze-colored tones on the glass. Not only that but there was also a dark plume of smoke coming out of the building. That smoke definitely hadn't been there before.

"Huh," she said, nudging Ahmed. "Check that out."

She pointed out the window toward the building and the plume of smoke. Ahmed leaned over, crowding her space as his forehead almost touched the glass. "Woah, that looks cool. It's almost like you can't even tell where the sky ends and the building begins!"

"Yes, but I was talking about the smoke. It seems weird, right?"

"Oh. I guess. I mean, are you sure it's smoke? Maybe it's steam or something. We have no idea what they do there. They could be doing about a hundred different things that would create steam. And they'd have to let it out of the building somehow."

"Yeah, but that's not steam. It's too dark. It's definitely smoke."

Ahmed looked at it a moment longer and then removed his head from the glass. "So, what if it is?" He chuckled and gave a shrug. "Boy, you're sure obsessed with that building, huh? I mean, it's cool-looking and all. And yeah, it might be the most interesting thing we've seen on this trip so far, but—"

Jenny stopped listening for a moment. As she'd been staring out at the building, she'd seen something else. It had been very brief, very small, and had only been there for a moment, but she was *sure* she'd seen it. A small explosion.

Or maybe just a flicker of sunlight off the glass, she thought.

No. She'd seen it just as clearly as she was seeing the grass, the open field, the bus seat and the setting sun.

"Ahmed! Something just...I think there was an explosion out there!"

"Where?" he said, excited and again turning to the window.

"Over at the building," Jenny answered.

"Oh," Ahmed said, not quite as excited anymore. "Really, Jenny, you need to give that building a break. I think you're trying to make it more interesting than it is just to give the trip some excitement."

"No, I'm not; I really saw it!"

"If you say so," he said with a lazy grin.

Jenny thought about arguing the point further but didn't see the need. After all, maybe she hadn't *really* seen an explosion. The building *was* reflecting the sky, and the sun *was* casting sparkles and glittering, dancing sparkles all along the glass. Maybe that was all she'd seen.

Jenny made herself turn away from the glass. She took her eyes away from the building, the smoke, and any other mysteries that might be on the other side of the island. Maybe Ahmed was right. Maybe she wanted to see those things just to liven this trip up a little.

But deep down, she couldn't help but wonder.

What was going on over in that building anyway? And who would build a huge structure like that here, on an island that hardly anyone ever visited?

CHAPTER THREE

The day had been tiring, and with a good dinner settled in her stomach, Jenny felt certain she'd get a good night's rest. She figured that she might have different feelings about Grovey Island tomorrow after some sleep. Maybe she was being too critical about the place because of Dr. Gaunt's boring teaching.

However, when night fell, Jenny found that she had trouble falling asleep. At first, she dozed in and out, not quite asleep but not awake, either. This only lasted a while, though, and she eventually found herself staring at the ceiling above her bed. She and the four other girls participating in the trip had been housed in a single dormitory with a shared bathroom. The room, just like the facility they were staying in, was very charming and peaceful. Jenny could hear the gentle crashing of waves outside. The window to the right of her bed showed a perfect night sky, full of twinkling stars.

She could hear the light snoring of one of her roommates, but otherwise, there was only the crashing of waves outside. She loved the sound and was certain it would help her fall back asleep, but that appeared to not be the case. Instead, she continued to stare up at the ceiling, her thoughts drifting back to the odd, glass building. She thought of how it seemed to almost blend into the sky. She thought of the plume of smoke and—

Her thoughts came to a halt when she heard another noise outside the bedroom window. Were those voices? Had she heard a man laughing? Maybe...but who would be out on the beach at such an hour?

Having already accepted that she wasn't going to fall asleep anytime soon, Jenny quietly got out of bed. She tiptoed over to the window and looked out into the night. The sea was very close; close enough that Jenny felt she could open the window, toss a rock, and hit the water. She looked out at the golden strip of beach that bordered the sea and saw the source of the voices.

There was a small group of teenagers out on the sand. There were six of them sitting around a small fire on the beach. One had an acoustic guitar in his hands. The others were listening to him play, laughing and joking. The strumming of the guitar was actually rather pleasant, but she thought it just wasn't the best time for it. People were trying to sleep, after all.

As she scowled in their direction, Jenny saw some motion out on the sea, close to the beach. It was a school of dolphins. She counted at least six, though they were moving so quickly, breaking in and out of the water, that it was hard to keep up with them. She wondered if they were responding to the music from the beach. She'd read somewhere that dolphins were very smart and incredibly playful. Seeing them, Jenny almost wished she was down there on the sand, in the dark beside the noisy teenagers.

Of course, the rules for the trip wouldn't allow such a thing. Besides, she was only twelve years old, and though she would admit it to no one—not even Ahmed—something about the sight of the sea at night sacred her. She couldn't see the horizon, and the water looked like very dark glass. There was no telling what sorts of horrors lurked under that sheet of black.

Jenny stepped away from the window, realizing that she'd given herself quite a scare. She gave the dolphins one last glance before returning to bed. Jenny lay back down and tried to bury her head under her pillow to block the sound of the teenagers, but it did no good. After a while, they were all she could hear; the sound of the sea was even blocked off by it.

Why was no one else bothered by their noise? Was she really the only one that was hearing them? She supposed the other girls were too deeply asleep to hear it. She wondered if Ahmed had heard them yet and if he, too, was unable to sleep. Good grief, why couldn't they just be quiet?

Then, suddenly, the music stopped. There was silence, but for just a moment.

It was broken by a scream...a very loud and horrified scream. And after that, there was only quiet. No teenage voices, no guitar, just the sound of waves lapping against the shore.

Jenny got out of bed, again looking at her sleeping roommates and wondering how they were sleeping through all of this. She peered through the window, down on the beach. To her surprise, the teenagers weren't there anymore. The little campfire was still burning, and she even saw the guitar lying abandoned in the sand. It was too far away to tell, but she thought the neck had been snapped off the body.

That scream, she thought. *Someone was really scared...*

She looked out at the sea and saw that even the

dolphins had disappeared. Whatever had scared the teens away had apparently frightened the dolphins, too. Jenny slowly backed away from the window, realizing that she was getting more and more scared by the moment. She nearly headed back to her bed to go and pull the covers over her head, but then another thought occurred to her.

Ahmed was very smart. Maybe he'd be able to figure out a logical explanation for what she'd seen. Jenny knew they weren't supposed to leave their rooms, but she considered this a special case. If something weird was going on at the beach, shouldn't someone else know about it? Maybe if she and Ahmed talked it out, they could figure out who might be the best person to inform.

Tiptoeing out of the room, Jenny quietly opened and closed the door. She stepped out into the dark hallway, the little lights along the wall glowing dimly. She knew the boys' room was at the other end of the hallway. Jenny walked quickly, a little ashamed that the weirdness on the beach now also had her scared of the dimly-lit hallway.

She knocked very lightly on the door. The chaperones and teachers were in the rooms between the boys' and girls' rooms, and the *last* thing she wanted to do was wake them up. Not until she knew for sure what was going on. When no one answered, Jenny gently opened the door. All the boys were asleep, and she could see Ahmed in a bed by a window.

Doing her best to ignore the smell of stinky feet and sweat, Jenny sneaked across the room and shook Ahmed awake. He looked up at her through half-closed eyes.

"Jenny?" he said sleepily. "What're you doing?"

"Ahmed, I just saw and heard the craziest thing! There were these teenagers down on the beach, and then—"

"Jenny, you realize you've woken me up, right?"

"Oh. Oh yeah. Sorry about that. But listen! There were teenagers out on the beach, but then I heard a scream and all the teenagers were gone. It was like something had taken them!"

"You were probably just dreaming. Now, I'm going back to sleep, and so should you. I'll see you at breakfast."

Jenny had another objection on her tongue, but Ahmed rolled over to face the wall. She stood by his bed for several seconds, frustrated and slightly angry. But before Jenny could get too angry, she was able to see things from Ahmed's perspective. She'd woken him up late at night and then bombarded him with a crazy story. She didn't blame him for being upset.

But she *had* seen the teenagers, and she *had* heard that scream. She knew it hadn't just been a dream. She made her way back to her room, replaying it all in her head. She lay back down in bed, and even though the only sound to reach her ears was the crashing of the waves down on the beach, Jenny couldn't get to sleep for a very long time.

CHAPTER FOUR

After a good night's rest, Jenny was able to mostly push the scream, the teenagers, and the abandoned fire and guitar out of her mind. She knew that it *had* really happened and hadn't been a dream but was now fairly certain whatever had happened hadn't been that big of a deal. Probably just unruly teenagers having some fun.

When she sat down across from Ahmed at breakfast, she put on her best friendly face. "Sorry about waking you up last night."

"Eh, it's okay. You seemed really worked up."

"Well, I did see and hear the things I told you about. But now I don't think it was that big of a deal."

"Yeah, I mean, it *is* a beach, right? There have to be some crazy visitors every now and then. Maybe you should report it to Dr. Gaunt. He and the other folks who run this program might want to know that noisy teenagers were out on the beach last night."

"Maybe," Jenny said. But really, she had no interest in having any sort of conversation with Dr. Gaunt. In fact, she was much more interested in the stack of waffles and syrup on her plate than anything that may or may not have happened last night.

When breakfast was over, all of the students were ushered out of the cafeteria toward the bus. The morning waiting for them outside was gorgeous, so bright and sunny that it was almost like something out of a cartoon. A lot of the other kids had started to chatter and talk with kids from different schools, but Jenny and Ahmed continued to stick together.

As the bus drove down a narrow lane that led across a moor, Dr. Gaunt stood up in the aisle to address the students.

"Today will be all about fungi," he said. "We will be collecting mushrooms and spores to take back to the lab and observe under microscopes. And if we have time, we may also start to look at the inner workings of grub worms!"

Jenny had no deep interest in fungus, but she thought it might be pretty cool to check them out under a microscope.

"So, I want everyone to buddy up," Gaunt continued. "Choose a partner. You will explore one of the more diverse regions of the island with that partner today and attempt to find the best specimens."

Jenny and Ahmed turned to one another. At the very same time, they both said: "Hey there, partner!"

The bus was filled with a flurry of conversation as the other students picked their partners. After another ten minutes, with all of the students paired up, the bus stopped at the edge of a swampy-looking forest. The students stepped off the bus one by one, led by Dr. Gaunt. The driver also left the bus. He was apparently helping Dr. Gaunt today. He was carrying several plastic containers, likely for the students to store their mushrooms and other icky things in.

"This way, children," Dr. Gaunt said, waving them into the forest.

A thin trail wound its way through the trees. It was the sort of path that most people would probably miss unless they were making a point to look for it.

The students all slipped into the forest with Dr. Gaunt leading them and the bus driver at the back, carrying the stack of containers. Jenny couldn't help but feel like a true adventurer as they walked through the forest. With flowering plants of all kinds, tall trees, and a wall of green as far as the eye could see, she felt as if she, Ahmed and all the rest of the kids were on an

25

expedition in an undiscovered land. They followed a narrow footpath that took them downhill, deep into the forest. They had to push through stringy vines that hung from the trees, and when Dr. Gaunt came to a stop, the forest was so thick that Jenny could barely see any patches of blue sky through the branches and leaves overhead.

"Now, students, I would like each of you to find one example of a Hericium Erinaceus and one example of a Cantharellus," Dr. Gaunt said. "You'll have exactly one hour to find these samples. I highly recommend not wandering too far to the north, as the ground can get quite swampy. I'd hate for you to lose a shoe."

As Dr. Gaunt continued to talk, Jenny thought she could hear a faint noise coming from very far away, deeper within the forest. It sounded like drums, a very slow beat that made her think of the teenagers playing music down on the beach last night.

Yeah, what happened to them anyway? she wondered. Being in this thick forest where she could barely even see the sky, it was a scary thought.

"Now," Dr. Gaunt continued, "as you're in pairs, I expect you to find *two* of each specimen."

He kept talking, pacing back and forth in front of

them, but Jenny barely heard him. She was too focused on that odd drumming sound that she was sure was getting closer. *Ba-doom. Ba-doom.*

Ahmed leaned over and whispered in her ear. "You hear that?"

"I do."

"What is it?"

Another kid beside them had noticed it as well. "It must be thunder. Maybe it's going to rain."

Jenny thought this might very well be the case. But the next time she heard it, she *felt* it, too. It now seemed that every student could hear it; they were all looking around, trying to figure out where the sound was coming from. The only person who seemed oblivious was Dr. Gaunt, who was far too busy listening to the sound of his own voice.

"...and if we finish up early, then we can venture out a bit further to find a specific species of moss that—"

Jenny raised her hand. Dr. Gaunt seemed excited to have a student ask a question. "Yes, young lady?"

"Sir... um... what's that noise?"

"Noise? What noise?"

Almost right away, the sound came again. *Ba-doom! Ba-doom!*

"That noise, sir."

Dr. Gaunt looked confused. He turned away from the students and looked out into the forest. The sound came again and then again. And while there was definitely a specific timing to it, almost like a beat, Jenny was quite sure it wasn't drums. As they all stared out into the forest, Jenny could see leaves shaking in the distance as if something was disturbing them.

"Is it an earthquake?" another of the students said.

"No, I don't believe so," Dr. Gaunt said. "Grovey Island hasn't had an earthquake for over two hundred—"

The noise came again, and this time there was a very noticeable shaking of the ground. More than that, though, there appeared to be something very large moving through the forest. Even the tops of the tallest trees swayed and shook.

Jenny could feel the shaking in her bones, and she was starting to feel very nervous. She was about to turn to Ahmed to tell him she thought they needed to run, but before she could say anything, the sound came once more. Everyone heard it, and a few kids were even holding on to one another for support as the ground shook.

But no one had time to focus on the noise this time. Everyone's eyes and attention had gone to the trees, where it seemed almost every branch was shifting and every leaf was moving. And as the students and Dr. Gaunt started to back away, the trees seemed to part. With her neck angled up, Jenny saw something enormous emerge from the trees. Branches were snapped in half, and leaves and twigs rained down.

Jenny knew that what she was seeing was impossible. An enormous head was sticking out of the trees above them. An enormous head with a long snout. It had small eyes, leathery skin and a *lot* of teeth.

It was a dinosaur. And not just any dinosaur, it was a—

"It's... it's a T-Rex!" Ahmed squealed.

Jenny knew this was true, but her brain kept telling her that it couldn't be real. After all, dinosaurs were extinct.

Apparently, this particular tyrannosaurus rex didn't know this because it was right there in front of them. It opened its enormous jaws and let out a roar. The entire world seemed to shake, and Jenny could feel her clothes being blown about as if a mighty wind had passed through the forest.

The students started screaming and running for their lives, some back for the bus and others blindly racing off into the forest. The bus driver dropped all of the containers and tripped over his own feet as he raced to get back to the bus. Ahmed was too terrified to move and just gazed up in terror at the T-Rex as Jenny tried to pull him away.

Dr. Gaunt looked up at the T-Rex, his eyes wide with wonder.

"Fascinating," he said. "Absolutely fasc—"

He didn't get to finish. Because at that moment, the T-Rex leaned down and devoured him. Dr. Gaunt was there one moment and simply gone the next. There was no blood, and the poor man didn't even have time to scream; the T-rex gobbled him up without much fuss, the same way Jenny might eat a peanut.

"We have to get out of here!" Jenny screamed.

Ahmed nodded, then the two of them ran off in the direction of the bus. They ran as quickly as they could, but after just a few seconds, the forest was filled with that sound again: *BA-DOOM! BA-DOOM! BA-DOOM!*

The T-rex was chasing them.

CHAPTER FIVE

"This can't be happening!" Ahmed screamed as they ran. "I mean, dinosaurs are extinct, right? And even if they *aren't,* how on earth has a dinosaur *that big* been hiding on this island?"

"I don't know," Jenny said. She swatted at a low-hanging branch that nearly whacked her in the face. "But I don't think I want to stick around to ask it!"

As they ran, the bus driver ran up beside them. He accidentally bumped into Ahmed. Ahmed fell to the ground with a yell, falling off to the side of the path. He tried to get up, but he'd gotten tangled in a thick cluster of vines hanging from a nearby tree. "Help!" he cried. "Jenny...help!

Jenny stopped and turned back to Ahmed. He had managed to free a leg, but now both his arms were tangled in the vines. And all the while, the *BA-DOOM* sound continued to fill the world. The forest shook, and the ground quaked. Jenny reached Ahmed and started tearing at the vines. They were very thick and felt rather slimy. It was hard for her to get a good grip on them. She turned back to the driver, still speeding ahead.

"Hey! Hey Mister," Jenny hollered. "Can you please help? You knocked my friend down, and now he's stuck!"

The driver stopped, but for only a moment. "I'm sorry," he said. "I can't stop. That thing..."

Suddenly the T-rex tore through the trees in front of the driver and let out another deafening roar.

"No," the driver whimpered. "No, no, no, no—"

And then the T-rex reached down and grabbed him in its jaws. The driver screamed as the dinosaur lifted him into the air, his legs sticking out of the beast's mouth.

Jenny quickly turned back to Ahmed and started tugging at the vines even harder than before. Behind her, she heard a sickening crunch and then an awful swallowing sound.

"Come on, come on!" Ahmed whispered.

The vines finally came loose, and Ahmed pulled his arms free. He jumped to his feet, and Jenny took him by the hand. She pulled him deeper into the woods, off of the path. They didn't dare look back to see if the T-rex had spotted them.

They leaped over fallen logs and dodged low-hanging branches, running as fast as they could. For a moment, they thought they were safe, but then they heard the sound of breaking trees and booming footsteps behind them. Jenny turned and screamed as she saw the T-rex rushing through the forest towards them. The thick trees were slowing it down, but it was catching up fast.

"Ahmed, it's chasing us!"

Still pulling Ahmed along by the hand, Jenny started descending a small hill. Jenny had no idea how long they'd been running, but it seemed this forest would never end. She'd never run so hard before, her feet slamming into the ground and her knees working like a machine.

She'd just started to worry that she wouldn't be able to run much longer when she saw a break in the trees just ahead. She saw a field of tall grass and a huge stretch of sky in the distance.

"If we come out of the forest, the T-rex will catch us for sure!" said Ahmed. "The only thing slowing it down is the trees."

"I'm not sure we've got much choice," said Jenny. "There's nowhere else to run."

The T-rex was too close behind for them to go in a different direction. They had no choice but to go straight ahead. They ran out of the forest onto the grassy field.

As they ran, Jenny dared another glance back over her shoulder. Thankfully the T-rex was struggling to get through the trees and the vines.

In the field, running was much easier. Without trees and fallen logs to dodge and leap over, they moved much faster. But just when things were starting to look up, there was an enormous crashing noise as the T-rex burst out of the forest behind them in an explosion of broken branches and leaves. It let out a monstrous roar, then came running after them.

Ahead, on the other side of the field, there was more forest. If they could reach it in time, they might be able to lose the T-rex in the trees, but the T-rex was closing in on them fast.

Jenny ran as fast as her legs would go, but she knew it wouldn't make any difference. In a few seconds, the T-rex would catch up with them, and then they'd be gobbled up like Dr. Gaunt and the bus driver.

And there was nothing they could do to stop it.

CHAPTER SIX

The booming footsteps coming from behind them were so close now that the ground was shaking, and it took all their concentration to keep running and not fall over.

"Ahmed...we're not going to make it are we?"

"I don't know," he said, and Jenny could tell he was doing everything he could to not seem scared. But she knew he was. She could see it in his eyes and hear it in the sound of his voice.

Jenny wondered how many more big footsteps they would hear before the T-rex caught up with them. She tried not to think about it, but she was expecting to feel the beast's huge jaws grab her at any moment.

Then she saw something very strange up ahead. Something was moving through the forest on the other side of the field. At first, she couldn't tell what it was exactly, but after a few seconds, she saw that it was a car—an SUV. It came out of the trees and tore through the tall grass, heading right for them. She could barely make out the shape of the driver behind the wheel, but they were honking their horn and flashing their lights at them.

Jenny had always been told not to get in a car with a stranger, but she thought this must be the exception. She and Ahmed ran towards the car, waving their hands and shouting. The T-rex was now so close that Jenny could feel its hot breath on the back of her neck.

As they got closer to the SUV, the driver skidded to a stop with his passenger door facing them. Jenny got a better look at the driver: it was an old man in a cowboy hat. He was waving them on quickly with one hand and opening up the passenger side door with the other.

Ahmed jumped into the car so quickly that his butt never touched the seat until he was fully inside. Jenny came in next, sliding beside him and shutting the door.

"You kids are fast; I'll give you that," the driver said. He slammed his foot down on the gas, and the SUV rocketed forward. Jenny looked out the back window just in time to see the T-rex lunge at them. Its jaws slammed shut, just missing the back of the car, and then it roared in frustration.

As the car sped away from the T-rex, Jenny took a moment to get a better look at the old man. He was somewhere between the age of her dad and her grandpa and had a thin gray beard. His hair was scraggly, but most of it was hidden by his hat.

"Hold on, you two," he said.

They had almost reached the edge of the field, the T-rex still hot on their tail. For a moment, Jenny was afraid the SUV was going to hit a tree, but then she saw the trail at the last minute. The SUV bounced and lurched a bit when the driver joined the path, but after that, it got smooth. Actually, if there hadn't been a T-rex chasing then, Jenny thought it might actually be fun.

The driver took sharp turns, barely missing trees and every now and then coming so close to them that Jenny would close her eyes. The SUV's engine roared as the tires bounced up and down the trail. After a while, Jenny realized that she could no longer hear the dinosaur's footsteps.

"I think we lost him," the driver said after a while. Still, he continued to zoom down the path, his eyes staring through the windshield with great focus and concentration. He didn't slow down for several minutes until they came to a small clearing in the woods.

A house sat in the clearing, as well as a small garden and a little shed. The door to the shed was opened, revealing an old lawnmower and a dirt bike that seemed to be lifted up slightly for repairs. The old man pulled up beside the house and cut the SUV off. He tilted his head, listening to the forest outside. He then opened his door, listened again, and nodded.

"It's okay," he said, looking into the SUV at Jenny and Ahmed. "We're safe for now. You two okay?"

"Yeah, I think so," Jenny said.

"Me, too," Ahmed answered. "And sir, please don't take this the wrong way, but...who the heck are you?"

The man only smiled and started walking toward the house. "Come on inside," he said. "You can have some lemonade and sandwiches, and I'll tell you everything."

CHAPTER SEVEN

The lemonade was the sweetest Jenny had ever tasted, but the bread for the peanut butter sandwiches was a little stale. Still, Jenny ate it happily. She was glad to have it because just a few minutes ago, she was sure she would end up in the bottom of a dinosaur's stomach and never eat anything again.

The driver of the SUV sat down at the table in the tiny kitchen, joining Jenny and Ahmed with his own glass of lemonade. The front door of the cabin led directly into the kitchen. The cabin itself was very small. There was the kitchen, a living room, one bathroom and one bedroom. Jenny guessed the old man lived here by himself.

"What's your name?" Jenny asked him.

"Jasper. And yours?"

"I'm Jenny," she said between bites of her sandwich.

"And I'm Ahmed," Ahmed added.

"Good to meet you both." He smiled at them and said: "So I guess that was your first time running away from a tyrannosaurus rex, huh?"

"Yep," said Ahmed. "And hopefully the last as well."

"But how did a T-rex even get here?" Jenny asked. "Dinosaurs have been extinct for millions of years!"

"You're right about that," Jasper said. "But this island...well, there have been strange things going on here recently."

"Well, yeah," Ahmed said. "Apparently, dinosaurs live here. That's *very* strange."

"Hey, wait," Jenny said. "Do you *live* here? Is this your house?"

"Yes, it is. There are actually quite a few people that live on the island. I think the last count of people living here totaled around two hundred. Most of the people who live here are farmers, like me."

"Have you seen dinosaurs here before?" Jenny asked.

"I haven't myself, but I've heard rumors. But never about anything that big."

"Where on earth did it come from?" Ahmed asked. He'd drained his lemonade and clutched the glass excitedly.

"Have you two seen the laboratory on the other side of the island?" Jasper asked.

"Are you talking about that really tall glass building?" asked Jenny.

"That's the one. It's pretty new. It's only been on the island for about five years, and when they built it, it came up *fast*. There was a really big fuss over it. None of the people that lived here wanted that ugly glass thing on our beautiful island, but the company that put it there had friends in high places, and a lot of money was spent to make sure it got built. And ever since it's been there, the island has seen its share of strange things. Nothing like what I saw chasing you two today, but strange all the same."

"What do they do in that building?" Ahmed asked.

"No one knows for sure. But everything was fine here on Grovey Island until that building showed up. Ever since it's been built, there have been earthquakes and strange noises here and there. Some farmers have even complained about missing sheep and cows. Shucks, just two weeks ago, a good friend of mine lost fourteen sheep overnight. My friend said he could have sworn he saw some huge beast racing across his back field, but I didn't believe him."

"A huge beast like a T-rex?" Ahmed asked.

"Maybe," Jasper shrugged. "Now...I suppose I need to figure out a way to get you kids back to your group. You were with that school trip, right?"

"Yes, sir," Jenny said. "But we can't go anywhere now. Not with that thing on the loose!"

"Well, I can't call anyone to come and get you," Jasper said. "The electricity has been out for about the last hour or so. No phone lines or internet, either."

"Do you think that big laboratory and the dinosaurs are connected somehow?" Ahmed asked.

"I'm sure of it. From what I can figure, there was some sort of incident over there at the laboratory last night. I was on my way home from the village and thought I heard sirens over there. When I passed by the road where you can get a clear look at the place, there were strange flickering lights inside—like emergency lights."

"And I saw some teenagers vanish on a beach last night," Jenny said. "There was a scream, and then they were all gone."

Jasper seemed to think all of this through as he looked at Jenny and Ahmed. Jenny thought he looked scared but also determined to help them.

"Do you think we could call my parents?" Jenny asked. "Maybe they could send help."

"Well, it's like I said...the phone lines are out."

"Don't you have a cellphone?"

"I do, but there's no service. See...that's another thing. From what I can tell, the entire island lost connection to the mainland sometime this morning. I can't help but wonder if the satellite tower we use for communicating with the mainland has been destroyed. Probably by the T-rex or one of his dinosaur buddies."

"So, what can we do?" Ahmed asked.

"Well, I think it's very risky to try to get you back to the rest of your group. Not with that thing running free. I think we should lay low, at least for tonight. Maybe some help from the mainland will have arrived by then."

"And what if it hasn't?" Jenny asked, nervous.

"I don't know," Jasper admitted. "But if there's no help from the mainland and we can't get you back to your group, I think we may have to venture out to the docks. We can put you on a boat and get you out of here."

Jenny and Ahmed nodded. Jenny wasn't a fan of waiting things out, but she thought it was the smartest move in this case. So, the three of them sat quietly at the table, so quiet that they could just about hear the noise of huge footsteps far off in the distance.

CHAPTER EIGHT

With no electricity and no internet, time passed very slowly in Jasper's cabin. Jasper continued to try the phone lines and his cellphone, but neither appeared to be working. The three of them played card games for a while but gave up on it. Knowing there was a T-rex running loose on the island made it hard to concentrate.

Also, Jenny still couldn't shake the images of Dr. Gaunt and the bus driver being eaten from her mind. Thinking about how close she and Ahmed had come to being gobbled up sent a shiver down her spine.

"Mr. Jasper, do you think they were keeping dinosaurs over in that building?" Jenny asked.

The old farmer shrugged. He looked tired and scared, probably even more worried than before now that he had two kids in his care.

"I can't see where else they must have come from. No one has ever really known what they do in that lab.

No one on the island ever sees the employees. They come in and out on boats or even helicopters sometimes. None of them live on the island, so it's all very secretive. Up until this morning, I was quite sure dinosaurs were extinct. But now that I know better...well, I suppose anything is possible."

As the day wore on, there were still no working phone lines, and the electricity was still out. This was made even more alarming when the sun began to set. When dusk fell across the island, it felt darker than it should in the absence of lights. Jasper lit a few candles on his kitchen table, but it wasn't quite the same.

"I'll leave it up to the two of you," Jasper said as he looked out across his darkening yard. "I can take you to the harbor now, or we can wait. I don't think I've heard any of those footsteps for an hour or so now."

"What do you think?" Ahmed asked Jenny.

"I'm not sure," Jenny said. "I don't like the idea of being out there when it's dark. I mean...are you sure it's okay if we stay here overnight, Mr. Jasper?"

"That will be fine with me...though I don't have a spare bedroom, so the two of you will have to sleep in the living room. One of you can have the couch, and the other can have a sleeping bag for the floor." He said all of this with a frown on his face as if he wished he could offer his visitors a bit more. "But hopefully, we'll wake to some good news in the morning. Maybe we can get you back to your group or out to the docks so you can get a boat out of here."

All the talk of home made Jenny miss her family. She had been so excited to be part of this trip, and now it had turned into a nightmare. Jenny would have given anything to be watching some TV with her mom and dad before going to bed. Thinking about all of this made her sad, so she did her best to pitch in and help Jasper as dusk faded quickly into night.

With no electricity, Jasper had to make a small campfire out in his front yard. He used it to heat up some soup and water for tea. Together, the three of them had soup and bread. They ate by candlelight at Jasper's kitchen table. While they ate, they continued to hear far-away roaring noises and the occasional sound of huge footsteps. From this far away, it sounded almost like thunder.

As the night wore on, with little hope of things being resolved before the morning, Jasper set up the couch for Jenny to sleep on. He gave Ahmed a fluffy sleeping bag so he could sleep on the living room floor.

With the entire house lit only by a single candle

from the kitchen, Jasper stood by the door to his bedroom and looked back at them. "I'm awfully sorry this is how your trip turned out—that you're stuck in a cabin with an old farmer."

"Are you kidding?" Ahmed said. "I'd much rather be in here with you than with that monster out there, running around all over the place."

"Yeah," Jenny agreed. "You saved our lives!"

Jasper smiled and let out a yawn. "Well, see if you can manage to get some sleep. I'll do everything I can to get you guys off of Grovey Island tomorrow."

With that, he walked into his bedroom and closed the door. The cabin went quiet for a moment, the only noise coming from the ticking clock in the kitchen and the crinkling of Ahmed's sleeping bag.

"Can you believe this?" Jenny asked quietly in the dark. "Actual dinosaurs!"

"Well, to be fair, there's only been the one," Ahmed said. "And that's more than enough for me!"

"Do you think the other students are okay?" Jenny asked.

"I don't know. I hope so. But even if they made it back to the bus, there was no bus driver. So...yeah, I'm not sure."

Jenny fretted over this. Sure, she'd never met any

of those kids until two days ago, but it pained her to think about them running and hiding on this strange island while a T-rex was on the loose, looking for snacks.

"Hey, Jenny?" Ahmed said softly.

"Yeah?"

"What if we can't make it to the docks tomorrow? What if we can't get on a boat, and we're stuck here?"

"Someone from the mainland will come eventually," she said. "They aren't just gonna forget about a load of kids on a school trip. But I think Mr. Jasper means what he says. I think he's going to do everything he can to make sure we get out of here."

"Yeah... hopefully. Well, good night, Jenny."

"Good night, Ahmed."

The cabin went quiet again, and within just a few minutes, Jenny could hear Ahmed snoring. She had no idea how he could sleep, knowing there was an actual living, breathing T-rex somewhere on the island. As for her, Jenny couldn't sleep at all. She was too scared and, yes, maybe even a bit excited.

After about half an hour or so, the candle in the kitchen had burnt out, and Jenny finally felt her eyes growing heavy and her thoughts becoming distant. Sleep was finally coming to her, and she was glad for it. That meant tomorrow would be here soon, that they may get off of the island and—

Suddenly she heard a noise coming from outside of the cabin. At first, it sounded like nothing more than a light scratch—maybe just the wind brushing a tree branch against the side of the house. But after a few moments, the noise grew louder and closer. Jenny sat up and looked into the kitchen, toward the front door.

The sound was coming from the other side of the door. Something was scratching against the wood.

Jenny opened her mouth to whisper to Ahmed, but she never got a chance. Before she could call out his name, the front door came crashing down with a loud, splintering bang.

CHAPTER NINE

For a moment, all Jenny could see was the night sky through the door. But then she saw a huge dark shape creep into the house.

"Jenny?" Ahmed muttered sleepily from the floor. The loud banging of the door flying open had clearly woken him up, too. "What's going on?"

"Sssh!" she whispered. She swung her legs over to the side of the couch, ready to run if she had to. Ahmed was fully awake now and was sitting up in his sleeping bag, looking in terror at the kitchen.

Jenny continued to stare at the door as the shape came further into the kitchen. Then a second shape came into the house behind it—and then a third. When the third one walked in, she could tell that whatever these shapes were, they could barely squeeze in through Jasper's doorway. The creatures began sniffing around the kitchen as if looking for something to eat.

Jenny could hear a low growling noise as the three shapes advanced. And then, as the leader of the trio stepped further into the cabin, it passed by the kitchen window. By the moonlight that came through the window, Jenny could now clearly see their intruders. Fear welled up inside her, and she did her best not to scream.

The intruders were dinosaurs. She wasn't sure what kind they were, but they were much smaller than the T-rex. In an odd sort of way, they resembled a duck that had been mixed with a lizard. They stood at about five or six feet, but they looked much larger in Jasper's tiny kitchen. Jenny knew a decent amount about dinosaurs, but she didn't know what species these were.

"Jenny," Ahmed gasped from the floor. "Those...those are austroraptors!"

The austroraptors, or whatever they were, hadn't spotted them just yet —they were still too busy exploring the kitchen.

"Quick, we need to hide before they come in here," Ahmed whispered, and he quickly crawled behind the couch. Jenny followed. She knew they should really warn Jasper, but if they tried to go across the room and open the old, creaky door to his bedroom, the austroraptors would definitely spot them.

Jenny hid behind the couch next to Ahmed, never taking her eyes off the austroraptors. One of them seemed to have found a scent to its liking on the kitchen floor. Another was sniffing at the candle Jasper had been burning for most of the night.

The space between the couch and the wall was tight but served as an effective hiding spot. The only issue, of course, was that if the dinosaurs spotted them, there would be nowhere to run in Jasper's tiny cabin.

For a moment, Jenny dared to hope that once the raptors had explored the kitchen, they'd go back the way they'd come, out of Jasper's front door and back into the night. But then the worst thing imaginable happened: the three austroraptors came into the living room.

Jenny had never been so scared before. She felt herself shaking and could also feel Ahmed trembling beside her. Jenny didn't dare look out from behind the couch, but she could hear the heavy footsteps of the austroraptors as they made their way through the living room, sniffing at the air and making their soft, growling noises as they looked the place over.

Without any warning, one of the austroraptors

nudged at the couch. The couch moved backward, squeezing Jenny and Ahmed against the wall. As Jenny and Ahmed scrunched up together, Ahmed let out a painful yelp.

The cabin went silent instantly as the austroraptors heard the noise and redirected their attention. With two huge strides, the lead austroraptor came around the side of the couch and looked down at them with its yellow, reptilian eyes.

Jenny felt as if she were paralyzed, frozen into place. But Ahmed didn't have that problem. In a flash of motion that was so fast that Jenny barely even saw it, Ahmed slid out of their hiding spot and went directly between the austroraptor's leg. The duck-like dinosaur opened its beaked mouth, filled with sharp teeth, and snapped at him. It missed Ahmed by less than three inches, its teeth sinking into the arm of the couch. Jenny could hear the wooden frame crack under the pressure of its jaws. When it pulled away, stuffing came out and floated in the air like snow.

While the austroraptor was confused and irritated about the lack of human boy in its mouth, Jenny vaulted over the couch and ran for the kitchen. However, before she had a chance to properly run ahead, she saw that the other two austroraptors had

Ahmed trapped. They'd cornered him just inside the kitchen. As one of them circled around to trap him, it knocked over Jasper's kitchen table.

Thinking as quickly as she could, Jenny reached out for anything she could use as a weapon. It just happened to be the lamp that sat on the small end table on the other end of the couch. She tore it free of the electrical outlet and, without really even thinking, chucked it hard toward the two austroraptors that had her friend cornered. As the lamp slammed into the back of one of the austroraptor's heads, the austroraptor that had bitten the couch lunged at her from behind. Jenny dodged the beast's huge jaws but then tripped over the coffee table and fell to the ground. She looked up at the austroraptor as it stood triumphantly over her, and she screamed in terror.

Just as Jenny lost all hope of escape, she heard a door swing open. Jasper rushed out of his bedroom holding a pitchfork, brandishing it at the raptor that stood over her. Oddly enough, Jenny's first thought was: *Who keeps a pitchfork in their bedroom?* But that was a question that could be answered later. For now, the important thing was that Jasper had a weapon.

The austroraptor standing next to Jenny lunged forward, hoping to attack first. But Jasper was deceptively fast. He plunged the pitchfork forward, and the prongs took the dinosaur high in its leg.

The austroraptor let out a howl of pain and anger. It was a noise that seemed to alert the other two. Their mouths cured back in angry grimaces as their third member hobbled backward, falling onto the couch.

Ahmed ran back into the living room, the other two raptors on his tail. Jasper brandished the pitchfork at them, keeping them at bay. They hissed with fury.

Jasper barely looked at Jenny and Ahmed as he focused on the raptors. "Both of you...go into my room and sneak out through the window. These things aren't going to let you out the front door."

"What about you?" Jenny asked.

"I'll be fine, just—"

One of the raptors made a small lunge at him, but Jasper wielded the pitchfork in its direction and it backed off.

"Go!" Jasper yelled.

Jenny and Ahmed looked at one another, nodded in unison, and ran for Jasper's bedroom. The wounded austroraptor tried to race after them, but it stumbled due to the injury Jasper had inflicted.

They ran into Jasper's bedroom and slammed the

door shut behind them. The room wasn't much: just a bed, a small dresser, and a few books scattered here and there. As they made their way to the window, Jenny noticed that a few of the books were about dinosaurs.

Ahmed opened the bedroom's only window and then stepped to the side to let Jenny go through the window first. As she started through, hoisting herself up and over the windowsill, a loud banging noise came from the living room. Then something heavy hit the wall, shaking the entire cabin.

"Come on," said Ahmed.

Jenny made her way out of the window, her feet coming down on the tall grass outside the cabin. Ahmed came over next, slipping out as if he'd exited a house through a window at night many times before. Just as they started to look around, everything still shrouded by nighttime shadows, Jasper came rushing into the bedroom, slamming the door shut behind him. Jenny watched him through the window. He came to the open window, tossed the pitchfork out to them, and then made his own way through the window. He didn't come out nearly as quickly or as easily as Jenny or Ahmed, but he was still pretty fast and agile for his age.

"Great job, kids," he said. "Now, to the car! We...hold on. Can either of your drive?"

"Um...no," Jenny said, a little embarrassed. "Why can't *you* drive?"

"I'm going to try to keep these things here while you escape."

"But you'll—" Jenny began.

"Just go, please! Trust me... I can handle myself. What about you, Ahmed? Can you drive?"

"Not really. I mean, I've done some simulator games and that sort of thing, but no *real* driving."

"You know how to start a car?" Jasper asked.

"Yes, sir."

"Then that will just have to do. Now get on out of here! I'll handle these monsters."

At that very same moment, one of the dinosaurs came crashing through the front door. It tore what remained of the door from the hinges and also took out a sizable chunk of the doorframe. It roared and instantly started coming for them. As Jasper stood his ground and brandished the pitchfork, Jenny and Ahmed took off running for the SUV.

"Do you really think you'll be able to do this?" Jenny asked.

"No idea," Ahmed said as he opened the driver's

side door and hopped in. "But I guess there's only one way to find out, right?"

He started the engine, and though it took some trial and error with the clutch and the gearshift, he finally got the SUV moving. Jenny looked back to see how Jasper was managing the austroraptors but couldn't see him. She could see the shadowy shapes of the raptors, but Jasper was blocked by their bodies.

"I feel bad for leaving him," Jenny said. "Ahmed, should we stay and help?"

"How?" Ahmed asked. "Besides...he told us twice that he could handle it. He seems like a pretty sharp guy. I think he'll be okay."

Jenny wasn't so sure, though. She could only look back into the darkness as Ahmed did his best to keep the SUV running, turning the headlights on as he sped down the winding trails of the island.

CHAPTER TEN

The ride was bumpy and quite hectic, but Jenny was impressed with how Ahmed was handling the SUV. The clutch groaned, and they nearly stalled out a few times, but Ahmed seemed to get the hang of it pretty quickly.

As they splashed through a shallow creek and bounded up a bumpy hill, Jenny was sure she heard a huge roar off in the distance. Then again, it could have been the rumbling of the SUV's engine, but she really didn't think so. It spooked her just enough to keep her eyes along the edge of the trail. The forest was so thick that she couldn't see into it. There was no telling what was watching from the trees, waiting to attack them.

"Woah!" Ahmed yelled, suddenly hitting the brakes.

Jenny held the dashboard to keep herself from flying forward. "What is it?"

But he didn't have to answer. Along the trail in

front of them, several small dinosaurs were crossing the dirt path. They didn't look dangerous. In fact, they were no larger than the dog Jenny's family owned. They ran on their back feet, their small arms held up in front of them. Their gray skin looked almost white in the glow of the headlights, and their tails whipped lazily behind them. Jenny counted four of them, but she could see the movement of others just to the sides of the trail as they romped into the forest.

"I think those are nanosauruses, right?" Jenny asked.

"Yeah, looks like it," Ahmed said. His eyes were wide with awe, but it was clear that he was sacred, too. Jenny could relate. That was exactly how she felt. It was *so cool* to see real, living dinosaurs, but she didn't have much time to appreciate the experience when she was being hunted down by them.

After the last of the nanosaurs had passed by, Ahmed put the SUV back into gear, and with a shaky lurch, the SUV blasted forward again. Jenny could tell that Ahmed was having the time of his life, tearing through the forest like he was in a real-life video game.

"Do you have any idea where the harbor is?" Ahmed yelled over the engine. "I wonder if we can get to those docks Jasper was talking about."

"Look!"

She pointed ahead of them, where the road forked off into two different directions. There was a wooden signpost with two signs at the point where the trail divided. One read *To Muir Village* and had an arrow pointing to the right. The other read *Harbor* and was pointing to the left.

"There's our answer," Ahmed said, quickly turning the steering wheel to the left. The SUV hugged the turn, and Ahmed straightened it out easily. He really was catching on quickly. Jenny supposed it had something to do with the threat of hungry dinosaurs all around them.

Within just a few minutes, the forest started to thin out to both sides of the trail. To the left, Jenny could see twinkling lights off in the distance. She wondered if they were close to the resort the students had been staying in. Ahmed brought them around another curb, rising slightly uphill. And as the hill came to a crest, emptying out onto flat land, they came completely out of the forest.

Neither of them was prepared for the sight ahead of them.

"Woah," Ahmed said.

Jenny wanted to say something, too, but her voice

seemed to be caught in her throat. She couldn't believe what she was seeing.

The trail through the forest had brought them to a wide-open field. There was open ground as far as her eyes could see. The trail was still there, straight ahead of them and turning slightly to the right. However, the trail was not what Jenny was focused on. Not at all.

The field was alive with more dinosaurs than she could count. The first one she saw was a brontosaurus. She couldn't help but smile at the sight of it. `Sure, it was enormous, but there was something beautiful about the way it slowly moved, its long neck gracefully moving its head. On the other side of the trail, she saw a small herd of triceratops. There were five of them in all, including one that looked like it might be a baby.

"Can you believe this?" Ahmed asked.

"No. No, I really can't!"

Jenny looked around wildly as Ahmed inched the SUV down the trail. She saw a stegosaurus romping in the field less than twenty feet away. Behind it were all manner of smaller dinosaurs that Jenny didn't even know the names of. She wasn't afraid, though. As far as she could tell, these were all herbivores; these were dinos that had no interest in hunting two random kids for dinner.

Overhead, several pterodactyls were flying by, taking stock of all that was happening below. Even though the night hid away some of the sight, Jenny was astounded by their huge wingspans.

"Jenny, look!" Ahmed shouted. "Over there! It's a gastonia! That's my favorite dinosaur!"

Jenny had heard the name before but couldn't recall what it was supposed to look like. She followed Ahmed's pointing finger and saw a heavily armored dinosaur walking low to the ground on stubby legs. Its back and tail were covered in what looked like spikes. It watched the van roll by with great interest but stayed in place.

"This is unbelievable!" Jenny said. "Do you think the other kids on the trip are getting to see any of this?"

"No way," Ahmed said with a nervous smile. "Not up close and personal like this!"

The SUV started to bounce violently, and it was only then that Ahmed realized that he'd been so distracted by the numerous dinosaurs that he'd taken his eyes off the trail. He sped up a bit as he righted the SUV back onto the road. Up ahead, a group of small dinosaurs crossed in front of them. They looked almost cute, no larger than a big lizard, really. Their tails were thick back by their rear legs but tapered off into a thin point, swaying in the air like that of a happy dog wagging its tail.

The trail veered further to the right and then stopped at an intersection. A sign to the side of the road told them that the harbor was to the right. When Ahmed took the turn, Jenny could see it. The outline of the building was visible because of several small lights along what she assumed was a dock. It was too dark to see much more than that, but she could easily imagine boats bobbing on water she couldn't yet see.

Then, as the field started to give way to a downward tilt, they could finally see the sea. It looked endless in the dark, only the white caps of small waves breaking the black apart. Again, though, the dinosaurs all around them kept Jenny's attention from anything else. She kept her eyes open for any dangerous ones but, thankfully, she couldn't see any. As for the T-rex, she wasn't worried about him for the moment. With his size, she was sure they'd hear and feel him before they saw him.

As they drew closer to the harbor, Jenny could see lots of movement in the darkness. She saw a door open up, spilling light out onto the walkway, and then the shapes of several people—and not just any people, but kids! It seemed that Ahmed had been wrong after all.

Their classmates *were* getting to see all of this up close and personal.

"Ahmed, look! It's all of the other students."

Ahmed's smile widened even more at the sight of the kids being ushered to safety. Somehow, he got the SUV to go even faster—a little too fast for Jenny's liking. She pressed back against her seat and gritted her teeth. "You sure you should be going so fast?"

"They're in trouble!" he said, nodding ahead to the harbor building.

"What? No...they're safe inside there."

"Yeah, but look at *that,*" he said, pointing up.

Jenny looked to the night sky and saw the shapes of at least four pterodactyls—then five, then six. And they were all headed for the harbor building. At first, she didn't understand why Ahmed was concerned. Inside the building, the students would be safe.

But then she saw the docks that were attached to the back of the building. She remembered the building and the docks being separated by a small ticketing office. If that was where the other students were headed and if they *didn't* know the pterodactyls were circling, they could walk out onto the docks and directly into danger. She knew that pterodactyls were carnivores—that they ate meat, especially fish and small animals—and they were easily big enough to swoop down and pull a kid up into the sky.

"We have to help them!" Jenny cried. "If they step out onto the dock, they won't stand a chance!"

"I know," Ahmed said. "Why do you think I'm driving so fast? Do you have any ideas?"

She tried her best to think of something, but all she could come up with was the simplest solution. As she watched two of their teachers hurry the last of the students inside, she could only shrug and offer the idea she had.

"Just beep the horn! Maybe it'll distract the pterodactyls. And if they come after us, you can outrun them in this, right?"

"I think so," Ahmed said. And then, with a frown, he added: "I *hope* so. Let's give it a try!"

They were close enough to the harbor that they could now see the shapes of five boats tied to the docks along the side. Jenny could even see the shapes of several people moving through the small windows.

Ahmed slammed his hand down on the SUV's horn. The noise was surprisingly loud, so loud that it made Jenny jump back in her seat. To her right, it also grabbed the attention of a triceratops. It looked up from where it was grazing in the grass and gave the

SUV a perplexed look as it sped by.

The horn also attracted the attention of the swooping pterodactyls. Almost at once, they all redirected their course. There was no real formation to them; they simply tilted their wings and came swirling back around in the direction of the SUV. And now that they were all headed straight for them, Jenny could count as many as ten.

"Well, I guess that worked!" Ahmed said.

He waited just a moment, continuing to beep the horn. He then took a hard left turn that bounced them off the trail and onto the field. The SUV almost seemed to run smoother on the grass, but Jenny could see that it was harder for Ahmed to control. She could feel the wheels slipping in the grass, causing Ahmed to work harder at the wheel.

Jenny looked back and saw that the pterodactyls were still coming after them. She could also just barely see the students and teachers hurrying out to the docks and toward the first boat. While she was happy to see that their plan had worked, they still needed to try to escape...again. First the T-rex, then austroraptors, and now these pterodactyls.

And this time, they didn't have Jasper to help them.

The SUV continued to rocket forward. Ahmed headed right back to the trees to trick the pterodactyls into flying into the forest. But as he turned the wheel to the left to get back onto the trail, the back end of the SUV spun around, and he lost control.

"Hold on!" he yelled as he did his best to straighten it out.

The SUV went spinning around in a full circle. The front end nearly clipped the right leg of a stegosaurus as it swung around. In the confusion, Jenny noticed that they were headed towards a tree—one of the few that sat out in the field. It got closer and closer, and by the time she double-checked to make sure she had buckled her seatbelt, she knew they were going to hit it.

"Ahmed, watch o—"

The front of the SUV struck the tree before she could get the last word out. Because they'd still been in a spin and Ahmed had been hitting the brakes, the impact wasn't too bad. Still, the front of the SUV crumpled up like an aluminum can, and a plume of steam rose up from the hood.

"You okay?" Jenny asked, looking over at her friend.

"Yeah, I think so," he said, though it was clear he

was shocked. He was looking around, dazed and perhaps a little dizzy from all of the spinning. "Now what?"

"With the SUV wrecked, I don't know that we have much choice," Jenny said. She looked down at the dock and then back up at the pterodactyls that seemed to have lost interest now that the honking noise of the car horn had stopped. Still, they couldn't just stay here.

"We have to run for the docks!" said Jenny.

"I was afraid you'd say that."

They both unbuckled and stepped out into the dark field. Dinosaurs grazed and walked all around them but seemed to pose no real threat. But the moment they started running, the shrieks from the sky told them that danger was on its way. The pterodactyls had turned around and were now coming directly for the two kids running across the field.

CHAPTER ELEVEN

The harbor seemed impossibly far away. Jenny wasn't sure she'd ever run so fast in her life as she darted past huge dinosaurs and groups of smaller ones. She nearly tripped over a small raptor, no larger than a house cat. Jenny wanted to observe it to see which species it might be, but she knew he had no time. She looked back over her shoulder and saw that the pterodactyls were already starting to swoop down on them.

There was no way they were going to make it. She guessed that within another ten seconds or so, she and Ahmed would be scooped up into the sky by the talons or beaks of one of those sky-bound monsters. The question, she supposed, was whether they'd be eaten or if the pterodactyls would just drop them to the ground, to their deaths. Another possibility was that they'd be brought back alive to be fed to the pterodactyls' young—but Jenny really didn't want to think about that.

"Ahmed...I don't think we're going to make it," she cried.

"I know...I...I..."

But just as Jenny was sure they'd be snapped up off the ground, a puttering noise filled the night. It could be heard even over the shrieks of the pterodactyls. When Jenny looked to her left, she watched as a single, bright light tore out of the forest. It was aimed directly at them and sent the pterodactyls scattering. They screeched in frustration and swooped away, disappearing over the trees.

"What *is* that?" Ahmed asked.

"I don't know," Jenny said, squinting to try to see the murky shape behind the light. "But I think...I think it's Jasper!"

Sure enough, as the light got closer, she could see Jasper behind the light. He was sitting on a raggedy old dirt bike. A wide grin spread across her mouth as she realized she'd seen that dirt bike before; it had been in Jasper's shed when he'd first brought them to his cabin.

He drew the bike up alongside them. The motor's idling was almost as loud as the dinosaurs all around them. Jenny saw that he had a few scratches on his face, maybe from driving through the forest or maybe from fighting off the austroraptors back at his cabin.

"Jasper, you saved us *again!*" Jenny cried.

"Yeah, and I was happy to do it! Now the two of you get moving...go get on that boat with the other kids!"

"What about you?" Ahmed asked.

"I need to see if anyone else needs rescuing. I have lots of friends on the island, and I'm not sure if they've all managed to escape yet. *Now go!*"

Jenny reached out and hugged Jasper while he still sat on the motorcycle. Then Ahmed and Jasper shook hands. "Be careful, both of you," Jasper said as he watched them rush off toward the harbor.

Jenny was in the lead, running for the building and hoping the boat wouldn't leave without them. She hollered and yelled for the other kids, the teachers and whoever was going to be driving the boat. But she knew no one could hear her. The noise from the dinosaurs was just too loud. And even as they ran along, there was another sound—a noise they'd heard before. And the moment Jenny heard it, her eyes went wide with fear.

"Do you hear that?" she asked, turning her head toward Ahmed as she ran.

"Yeah," Ahmed said nervously.

It was a booming noise that they could barely hear over all of the other dinosaur commotion. It was coming from directly behind them, in the same direction the pterodactyls had flown off to. When Jenny turned to look back over her shoulder, she saw that the pterodactyls were flying back out towards the field. Only this time, they weren't flying on the attack; now, they looked to be retreating from something.

And with another booming noise that filled the field, Jenny saw why. She saw that her guess had been right.

The booming noises were the footsteps of a tyrannosaurus rex. Jenny saw it come tearing out of the woods, stomping across the field with its enormous feet. Jenny had no idea *how* she knew this to be true, but she was certain it was the same T-rex that had terrorized them yesterday when all of this craziness started. To think that Dr. Gaunt and their bus driver were very likely digesting in the belly of this dinosaur was creepy.

Jenny ran even faster than before. She ran so fast that she nearly tripped over her own feet. She dared one more glance over her shoulder as she and Ahmed drew closer to the harbor and watched in terror as the T-rex opened its massive jaws and gulped down one of the fleeing pterodactyls. Another of the flying bests tried attacking the T-rex from behind, but it quickly turned its huge head and had that one for a snack, too. Jenny watched as one of its wings hung from the T-rex's jaws, only to be swallowed down a moment later.

"Oh my gosh, Ahmed...*RUN!*"

But Ahmed didn't need to be told. He was running just as fast as she was, his feet little more than a blur beneath him. Behind them, the booming sounds continued as the T-rex came stomping further across the field—directly in Jenny and Ahmed's direction. It was like the T-rex wasn't just hunting them—it wanted revenge on them for the way they'd escaped from it before.

Thankfully at that moment, two more pterodactyls swooped down and started pecking at the T-rex, distracting it long enough for Jenny and Ahmed to escape.

They came to the bottom of the field, where the only thing separating them from the boats and the sea was the small harbor building. They dashed through the front doors and found the place totally empty. Anyone who had been inside was likely in one of the boats, ready to get off this crazy island. With the next *boom*, the overhead lights flickered. In the back of the building, a window cracked, and a picture fell from the wall.

The ticket counter was at the back of the building, down a flight of stairs. But even as they went down the stairs, it was clear that this part of the building had been emptied, too. A door to the back led out into the night—but more importantly, to the docks and the boats.

"Come on!" Ahmed yelled as he reached the bottom of the stairs. He raced across the wide hallway, and when he came to the door, he held it open for Jenny. When she passed through, she could smell the sea right away. She could also hear the revving of a boat engine and the nervous chatter of several kids carried on the wind.

Jenny looked out and saw that the only boat moving was the one closest to them. However, the bad news was that it had already been untied from the dock and was slowly making its way out to sea. But it was only a few feet away from the dock. Maybe if they jumped, they'd make it. Or, if they didn't, they'd end up in the water. And she didn't even want to think of what sort of prehistoric creatures might be swirling around down there.

"We're going to have to jump!" Jenny said.

Again, Ahmed already seemed to be way ahead of her. He was angling toward the edge of the dock, ready to leap across the open water into the boat. It was a small boat, and several of the kids they'd come on this trip with were crowded together on the deck, watching the island slowly drift away from them. When they saw Jenny and Ahmed, they started shouting at the teachers and the driver. Others clapped and waved, cheering them on.

Ahmed came to the edge of the dock and jumped without thinking. He made it quite easily, falling right into the back of the boat. Jenny came next, and when she jumped, there was a sickening moment where she didn't think she was going to make it. When she came down, her legs struck the side of the boat, and she almost fell backward into the water. But Ahmed's hands were there right away, reaching over the boat to help pull her in.

"That was *close,*" Ahmed said.

"Tell me about it," Jenny said, rubbing at her aching legs.

The other kids were still screaming, pointing back to the island. Jenny stood and looked, terrified at what she saw. The T-rex had made it to the harbor, and even as they watched, it barged into the building. The entire harbor seemed to explode in a cloud of glass, bricks, and dust. And then, to Jenny's horror, the T-rex emerged from the dust and began charging down the docks towards them.

The wooden docks began to strain under the beast's enormous weight, and for a moment, Jenny thought the T-rex was going to fall into the water. Behind her, one of the other students asked: "Can a T-rex swim?"

Jenny wasn't sure of the answer, so she looked at Ahmed. He wasn't saying anything, but he was nodding—nodding to say yes, a tyrannosaurus rex could swim.

Suddenly the docks collapsed, and the T-rex fell into the water. For one joyous moment, Jenny thought it was defeated at last, but then the top of the T-rex's enormous head emerged from the dark water. For a moment, it was still, but then it slowly began to move towards the boat. And suddenly, their boat didn't seem as safe, and their escape did not seem so certain.

CHAPTER TWELVE

Enormous waves started slapping against the side of the boat as the T-rex came after them, swimming through the water like a crocodile, with its legs together and its tail moving side to side. The boat was tossed, and the kids and teachers started to scream. There were only three teachers with them, and they were working hard to get all the students to the back of the boat. But that was easier said than done; while the sight of the T-rex chasing after them was horrifying, it was also very hard to look away.

Jenny guessed that the monster was no less than thirty feet away from them. She could even see its eyes and the close-cropped rows of its jagged teeth. It seemed to be making its way through the water with ease.

A huge wave came slamming against the side of the boat. All of the kids were soaked. A few of them were even knocked off their feet. Jenny looked back to the T-rex and saw that it was closer now.

As it swam forward, she could only see its head. Its nostrils flared, and its eyes stared directly at them as if it could already imagine what they all tasted like. To Jenny's surprise, one of the teachers came running to the back of the boat. It was a short, stout woman, and though she looked terrified, Jenny could see her determination. She was, after all, a teacher, and she had a duty to protect the students. The teacher reached to the far side along the back of the boat and pulled a wooden oar out. She reached out with it and slapped at the T-rex. To Jenny, it seemed like a foolish thing to do. But it also clued her in to just how close the monster was to their boat. The teacher could *almost* touch it with the oar. It was *that* close.

The teacher yelled out and slapped out with the oar again, leaning so tightly to the back of the boat that she nearly fell into the water. This time, the oar whacked the T-rex on the nose. It made a harsh roaring noise that came from under the water in a cloud of bubbles. It then lifted its head, its enormous jaws springing open. Jenny could see into its mouth, each and every one of its sharp teeth and its deep, dark throat.

She started to stumbled backward in fright,

reaching out and taking Ahmed with her. The teacher now stood there with the oar in her hand, looking into that wide-open mouth in horror.

The T-rex chomped down hard, crunching the back of the boat and reducing it to splinters. The entire boat shook and trembled. Water started to wash up onto the deck.

"This isn't good," Ahmed yelled. "He's either going to eat us, or the boat is going to sink!"

Jenny realized just how unfortunately true this was. She ran to the side of the boat, angling closer to the front where the other kids were packed tightly, grouped together and screaming. Jenny could just see the mainland, really just a few twinkling lights. Even when they got there (*if* they made it there), her home was a four-hour drive away. Home had never seemed so distant as she saw those faint lights along the mainland, and she was starting to worry she might never see it again.

Ahmed caught up to her as the boat sputtered slowly, the back end demolished. The T-rex looked annoyed: apparently, wood, paint, and part of a propeller weren't to his tastes. He was distracted, but Jenny knew it wouldn't be long before the dinosaur turned his attention back to them.

With the back end of the boat torn apart and the propellers destroyed, the boat wasn't moving anymore. Two of the teachers began to row using the oars, but there was no way they could escape the T-rex now. And the next time it opened its mouth, Jenny was afraid that the boat and all of the students and teachers would go down with it. And this time, Jasper wasn't going to be around to save them.

Jenny and Ahmed cowered together at the front of the boat with the other students. The deck was wet, making it hard to keep their footing. Jenny could feel the boat tilting as the shattered back end started to sink. One of the teachers was running around handing out life jackets. Jenny understood why she was doing this but didn't think it would do any good. If they *did* end up in the water, the life jackets would make it that much easier for the T-rex to find them.

With certain death looming, Jenny reached out and took Ahmed's hand. This was it...this was how it was going to end. She'd never see her home again, never see her parents again. The T-rex turned and began swimming towards them once more. The kids all began to scream. If Jenny hadn't been paralyzed by fear, she would have screamed too.

A flicker of blue erupted out of the water directly

between the back of the sinking boat and the T-rex. Just as Jenny's eyes had seen this, another flash came out of the water. It took her a moment to understand that she wasn't seeing flashes of light but actual creatures that were jumping up out of the water.

"Jenny!" Ahmed said. "Are those...are those dolphins?"

Jenny smiled as another soft blue flash came out of the water, then another. "Yeah! Yeah, they are!"

A whole pod of dolphins seemed to be swimming between the back of the boat and the T-rex. They were just fast enough to avoid its snapping teeth and clever enough to get in its way. As Jenny watched, a pair of dolphins leaped up out of the sea and slammed into the side of the T-rex's head. Their noses acted like little clubs, pummeling the T-rex and making him roar in frustration.

Two more came out of the water on the other side of its face and did the same thing. More dolphins than Jenny could count were zipping around the T-rex in the water. The dinosaur could easily push past them, but they slowed him down just enough for the boat to finally get some distance from it.

Behind them, Jenny heard a very loud honking noise. She turned around and saw that the ferry that had left ahead of their boat had turned around to rescue them. Already, it was pulling in beside their boat. One of the crewmen on the ferry was letting down their ramp and setting it up against the side of the boat.

"Come on, children!" one of the teachers said. "One by one, on the ramp!"

The kids obeyed and created a single file line at the front of the boat as they waited to get on the ferry. Some were cheering, but some still seemed pretty terrified of what was happening. They were, after all, on a sinking ship—a ship that was sinking because a real-life dinosaur had taken a bite out of it. One by one, they made their way across the ramp and onto the ferry. All the while, the brave dolphins continued to attack the T-rex. Jenny could even hear them making noises. In their cute dolphin language, it almost seemed as if they were laughing.

"Come on, you two!" the teacher yelled. It was the same woman who had struck the T-rex with the oar. She was completely soaked but still had that fiery determination in her eyes.

It was strange, but Jenny wasn't quite ready to leave. She wanted to keep watching the dolphins assault the T-rex. They'd moved further away from the dinosaur, but she could clearly see that the dolphins were driving the T-rex back toward the island. Jenny gave Grovey island one last look. She hoped that Jasper was safe, whatever he was up to.

She knew he wouldn't be able to see it, but she waved goodbye anyway. And then, still holding Ahmed's hand, she walked up the ramp. The teacher helped them up and along, and before she knew it, Jenny was standing on the much more secure flooring of the ferry. Once everyone was on board, the crewman quickly drew the ramp back in, and the ferry sped off.

Jenny and Ahmed stood at the back of the boat and looked out. They could still see the T-rex and the dolphins battling it out, the T-rex being pushed even farther back to the island. Behind this battle, Jenny could just make out the huge shapes of other dinosaurs in the night.

And further away to the right, on the other side of the island, something flickered. Jenny looked in that direction, catching the moon shining off the corner of the large, glass building. She knew the sudden appearance of the dinosaurs had something to do with that strange building and the mystery of it all was too much to ignore.

But it would have to remain a mystery as the ferry

puttered along the sea, getting closer and closer to the soft lights of the mainland

CHAPTER THIRTEEN

The next day, Jenny and Ahmed spent most of their time sitting behind a large desk, speaking to someone from the government. Jenny wasn't sure if it was a police officer, a detective, or maybe even someone from the FBI or MI6 or an organization like that. Whoever it was, they asked Jenny and Ahmed tons of questions about what happened on Grovey Island.

It wasn't so bad, really. Honestly, it was sort of exciting. There were police, phone calls, new clothes to change out of their wet ones, news crews, cameras, and a very nice lady in uniform who kept bringing Jenny, Ahmed, and all of the other students cups of hot chocolate.

She and Ahmed had remained together, and every time they were interviewed, it was as a pair. After all, they had one of the craziest stories of all to tell. They'd narrowly escaped three different kinds of dinosaurs. The people giving the interviews seemed especially impressed by their escape from Jasper's cabin while the austroraptors had been on the prowl.

They were in the room alone now, Jenny staring at the many printed pages that contained their story. When the door to the office opened up, a tall man wearing a military uniform entered.

"Jennifer and Ahmed, right?"

"Yes, sir," Jenny said.

"We've contacted your parents, and they will be here within a few hours. If you like, you can speak to them on the phone."

"Sure, that would be great," Ahmed said.

"Come this way," the man said. He grinned at them and added: "I hear the two of you had some incredible adventures on that island."

"We sure did," Jenny said.

"Sounds like you're both very lucky to be alive."

The man led them to another office, where two other students sat at tables. They were both talking on cell phones, probably to their parents, Jenny thought. As the military man led them to two other tables, Jenny glanced through a long window that looked out onto the lobby of the budling. There were all sorts of news crews and policemen out there, lots of people having conversations with one another and a lot of movement. But on the right side of that room, speaking very heatedly with a policeman, was a face she knew. Jenny smiled and clapped her hands in excitement. She forgot about making the phone call and ran to the door instead.

"Ahmed, it's Jasper!" she cried. "Jasper's here!"

They both rushed out and found Jasper mixed up in the big group of people. When he saw them coming, he smiled and wrapped them both up in a big hug.

"I knew you two would make it! You're tough and pretty darn smart."

"Jasper, how'd you get here?" Ahmed asked.

"The military sent a boat over this morning and evacuated all the remaining folks on the island."

"And you're okay?" Jenny asked.

"Oh, for sure! A little tired, but that's about it. I was—"

He stopped here and tilted his head to the side. Jenny noticed that he wasn't the only one. Several people all around them in the main lobby had stopped talking. A few had walked over to the large windows.

And that's when she heard the scratching noise. It came from outside, something grazing against the glass of the window. Jenny looked out through the window just as several people not too far away started to scream.

All around her, the place seemed to go into a frenzy. People were screaming; others were running and ducking down. The soldiers who had guns took out their weapons.

"What in the world?" Ahmed said.

Looking through the glass, Jenny saw what had scared everyone.

Just outside of the building, a single austroraptor was looking in. It was running its claws along the window, trying to figure out how to get in. Further behind it, coming down the street, Jenny saw several more. She wasn't sure how many there were, but she counted at least ten. And they were running directly for the building.

Somehow, the dinosaurs had made their way to the mainland. She backed up into Ahmed, and standing just behind them, Jasper was also looking out.

The lobby was filled with panic and screams as some people ran for safety. A few seconds later, with the austroraptors still surging forward, a loud siren sounded off inside the building. Shots were fired. And even as Jasper started to pull Jenny and Ahmed away from the window, Jenny had a very bad feeling.

If the austroraptors had made it across to the mainland, what else might have also made the journey? And where were they supposed to go now? Because if the dinosaurs had escaped the island, that could only mean one thing.

Now, nowhere was safe.

Printed in Great Britain
by Amazon

19439868R00058